THE
WHISPER
THAT
REPLACED
GOD

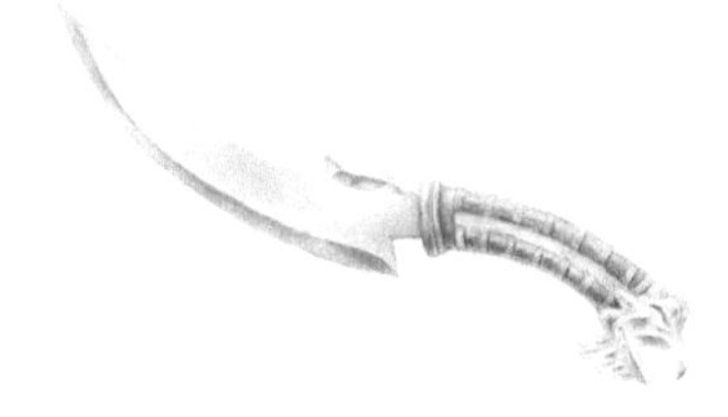

TIMOTHY WOLFF

Partnered with Willow Wraith Press.
Visit our website at Willowwraithpress.com.

ISBN: (Paperback)
ISBN: 979-8-9907730-2-8 (eBook)
ISBN: 979-8-9907730-4-2 (Audiobook)

Front cover image by Alejandro Colucci
Edited by Jonathan Oliver
Title page image by Coe Landsell
Book design by Lorna Reid

First printing edition 2024.

CHAPTER I

THE GIFT OF SILENCE

hile the cost to enter Eleanor's brothel was two silver, there was an additional price. It wasn't written on the door, but rest assured, anyone who stepped inside would never find heaven. Such a terrible toll never bothered me, for I had paid it long before tonight. In the way one could never threaten a headless man with decapitation, I would never see, feel, or touch whatever awaited me beyond this life. In a way I cannot describe, that alone was hell.

I handed my silver to Beatrice, headmistress of Eleanor's. Brothels always have a bizarre hierarchy. It would seem most questionable establishments are named in honor of people who, in fact, do not exist.

"Welcome, Lord Mute!" she said with a smile, wisely not referring to me as Prince. "Shall I gather Dorothy and prepare the usual accommodations?"

Usual? Perhaps I had come here too often. Never a good sign to hold any sort of usual in a den of vice. But how could I resist Dorothy? She was my favorite, and she favored my gold. The perfect transaction. I had learned more about supply and demand from the lower half of her body than any textbook of economics. "Sorry, Love. Not that sort of evening."

"Indeed," said Beatrice, never breaking her smile. And believe me, I checked for cracks. Very few people could learn there would soon be a murder in their establishment and not show a reaction. But ah, Beatrice. Women stuck with the worst of men often become the best of actors.

I approached an open chair without escort, signaling one of the women to bring me a chalice of wine. Most men referred to them as ladies of the evening, though I always found the phrase absurd. It's not like they're vampires. Many bizarre sights, sounds and…smells made their presence known as I took my seat. I will do you a courtesy and leave out the less desirable details.

Like an outbreak of plague, the whispers began as soon as I got comfortable. I didn't need to listen to the words in order to hear them. The intelligent ones would know the Gift of Silence would soon be unleashed. In such moments, I regretted the burden of being forced to wear a mask. The irony of masks is how their purpose of anonymity creates the opposite effect when there's only one in the room.

My brother, King Merrick Elmere of Balewind, the closest thing to God I ever knew, had made my assignment clear. Tonight, Emissary Archibald would fall to my dagger. He would die screaming and, thanks to the Gift of Silence, no one would hear a thing.

On the second floor was Archibald's…room? Quarters? Office of negotiation? Not really sure what to call it, but it was guarded by two very distracted guards. Similar to masks, guards can create the opposite of their intended effect. Archibald was "safe," but guards around a person or place will always create a perception of value for thieves or—in this case—murderers to take notice.

And believe me, I noticed.

I sipped my wine. It was shamelessly powerful. To be honest, it was probably just alcohol with red food coloring. Dens of vice are most efficient without the inconvenience of clarity. Interesting things occur when men are separated from their inhibitions. What a pity: I always favored wine before an assassination. For the uninitiated, several feelings arise when a man dies in your arms. With enough alcohol, you feel none of them until tomorrow. With more than enough alcohol, tomorrow can be delayed for quite a while.

A man's giggle interrupted my focus. I *hate* when grown men giggle. But more importantly, a woman's fake giggle followed. I knew it was fake because it was the voice of Dorothy. She only giggled when she was with me and, right now, she was with my uncle, so each giggle was a fake, a fraud, a sham, or whatever your word of choice for such an outrageous occasion. Dorothy was mine and mine alone. Who would dare tempt the wrath of the Silent God's chosen one?

Ah, Uncle Gunther. Brother to my father, the fallen king. An uncle who never loved me. An uncle who touched *my* Dorothy. His hands groped her, touching her in places I will *not* describe, doing things I will *not* explain, telling her things I will *not* repeat.

I drank the rest of my wine and did not flinch despite the awful taste. Alcohol's only weakness happens to be time. I didn't want to feel anything, and I didn't want to feel anything now. Not tonight, not in twenty minutes, but now. Daggers don't share that weakness. A dagger in the correct location can make a man fade before he ever notices what's happening. A feat I was about to demonstrate on Uncle Gunther. But first…

I closed my eyes, cleared my mind, and focused on nothing. "*Hush*," I whispered, then the room went deaf.

My eyes could best explain the aftermath of Eleanor's without sound. Chairs and tables knocked about, wine spilled over—the dripping red liquid a prelude for what was to come. Patrons and entertainers alike rushed towards the exit. It was like they had died but never lived, trying to scream and failing to whisper. Let them suffer the intimacy of silence. Let them hear the world in the way a blind man views it. I doubt anyone makes a quantitative ranking of their five senses. Like anything else, the quickest way to learn something's value is to take it away. I always found it humorous how people grab their ears in the wake of silence. It was a total collapse of equilibrium, a complete denial that something they had taken for granted was now lost. Their hearing would eventually return. Usually.

There were two paths. The stairs would lead to Emissary Archibald. I could slay him, remain in my king brother's favor, and continue to act as the shamed assassin prince for Balewind. The other path…was Dorothy. I could slay my uncle and ride off into midnight with my paramour. She would hug me, kiss me, provide me with other services I will not describe, and thank me every waking morning for how I had enriched her life. She would be so grateful, I would no longer have to lavish her with gold.

This tale would be much shorter if I had chosen the first option.

Uncle cocked his head as I approached. Was it delusion? He pointed upstairs and yelled. Despite the silence, I could still see the strain on his throat. Did he think I was craven? Confused? Mad?

Mad. Now there was a thought.

Like most mistakes, it was the easiest decision of my life. I could only guess if Uncle had chosen Dorothy to spite me, or if tonight was an unfortunate coincidence of chasing a red-haired goddess through the gates of oblivion. To be fair, I never asked, instead tearing my dagger into his throat. Ah, to finally end a man I despised. It felt better than expected, so I stabbed him again. Then again. Again. Again.

Again.

Blood splattered against my mask, fortunately missing my eye holes. To lose sound was one matter, but sight as well? It would have been intelligent to leave in haste, but I couldn't help but stare at my fallen uncle. Ah, that feeling. The most damnable of feelings: regret.

No, not for Uncle, but for the life I had thrown away. I would never see Brother Dearest again unless it was moments before my execution. To flee would be the obvious choice, but what of Dorothy? How would she manage without me? She must have known I did all of this for her. I was her knight in shining armor who happened to wear a mask, who happened to be covered in her patron's blood. Hopefully, Uncle had paid her first.

I reached out my hand and mouthed, "Join me, Darling." Unfortunately, Dorothy kept her gaze on the dead man beneath us. How tragic for such beautiful eyes to linger upon a catastrophe. There was no time to wait. I grabbed her hand and pulled her forward. Stop, I know what you're thinking, but it was for her own good. I assure you, once Dorothy had a moment to collect her thoughts, she would realize what a joyous occasion tonight was.

Or not?

Dorothy slammed a chalice into the side of my head. I saw it coming but was too disappointed to react. The physical pain was limited, but my heart may as well have been stretched upon the rack. What caused such madness? Shock? Of course! It was shock and nothing more. Shock and nothing more. If only I could explain the scenario to my future wife. What an irony for the Gift of Silence to deny me the opportunity.

Guards rushed down the stairs from my peripheral vision. I could have killed most of them, but not all of them, so by that measure, it didn't matter. Still, there was no choice but to try. I tugged to create distance, but Dorothy stood her ground, latching onto my arm in pure madness. Ah, poor Dorothy. If my fallen uncle was a strain upon the heart, these men I was about to slay would be a recurring nightmare.

I assumed they knew my identity, so why did they attack? In

fact, I never made any attempt on the emissary's life. One would think they had been awaiting my arrival. Rather odd, really.

And unfortunate.

To be quite honest, they beat me with a wrath I fail to adequately describe with a metaphor. The only saving grace was they couldn't hear me scream. Silence was indeed a worthy ally. Shame often needs sound to come to fruition—and I had lots of shame to offer.

One of the guards grabbed Dorothy. I forced myself up, gritting my teeth through the privacy of my mask, then was thoroughly beaten again. They must have had orders to preserve my life, for while some unfortunate kicks hit me in unfortunate locations, nothing sharp ever pierced my skin.

Aside from Uncle, the only thing slain tonight was my pride. It was a shattered husk, a homage to failure, a terrible fate for a prince who had been destined to wear a crown but, instead, settled for a dagger.

At ease, Darling, I thought, as the world went dark. Not tonight, but eventually, on the grandest of days, we would live happily ever after.

Oh Brother Dearest, king of kings, what shame had I inflicted upon us all?

CHAPTER 2

LET THE HEAVENS SCREAM OUR NAMES

 always favored the snow. Not for the luscious texture. Not in the wonder that no two snowflakes ever appear the same. Not in the beauty of watching nature itself fall from the sky, only to melt within the gap of my fingers. Simply enough, I favored the snow because it made other people unhappy.

So one could imagine my surprise to awake to nothing but smiles and laughter. It hadn't been snowing at home, so perhaps I was heading east towards the kingdom of Ganfren. More importantly: I was alive. But why was I alive? Where was I going? Why was I within a cart? Obviously, quite some time had passed since my brothel debauchery. Drugs perhaps? I never favored lies, so I'll be honest and admit I still don't know. Rather rude for my captors not to offer me a clock, a watch, or some other construct to measure the finest human construct.

"Hey Boss, the prince is awake," a ruffian said. I could practically hear the lack of education linger upon his voice. It took a moment to realize his unfortunate voice meant the Gift of Silence had ended.

"Water…May I trouble you for some water?" I asked. Captive or not, it was a reasonable request.

My captors did not seem to agree. I was beaten again quite thoroughly. This time, unfortunately, nothing hid my screams.

"Halt!" a new ruffian said. He was probably the leader since they begrudgingly obeyed. "King was clear on delivery terms. We only get half the gold if he's dead. I didn't come all this way to lose an entire decade of wages."

"Can we at least have a go at the woman?"

Dorothy screamed from the back of the cart. I never favored loud sounds, let alone one from my love. Fortunately, I could end it all with a whisper. I took a deep breath, closed my eyes, and—

The leader pushed a cup of water into my hand. He leaned in and whispered, "Don't be so quick to call upon the silence. Stay calm and let words work their magic." Up close, the man smelled like the later stages of depression, despite his toothless smile. He stood straight and yelled, "Leave her. When we get our payment, you'll have enough gold to drown in whores, and perhaps enough to cure the diseases they give you."

Whore. A word I despised. A word often used by men to describe women who show them no interest. If this brute was suggesting my Dorothy was anything less than perfect…well, I would follow his advice. When the time was right, I would allow sound the opportunity to give life to their screams.

While my mask hid the vehemence of my scowl, the man must have realized he held my ire. He sat next to me and flashed that miserable, toothless grin. "Sheathe those daggers in your eyes, friend. You should be kissing my ass in gratitude. But really, I don't get it. Why her? You should see the ladies in Ganfren. They can do things with their tongue that would make any priest renounce their faith."

"Why her?" I said, tilting my mask to look him in the eyes. Obviously, the man was a fool; his lack of intelligence made the question nearly impossible to answer. How does one describe what beauty is to a potato? "If you even have to inquire, the truth is far beyond your scope of reality. Dorothy is perfection incarnate. If you can look upon her without trembling, you may as well forfeit your eyes, for you see nothing."

I wasn't sure why my response provoked laughter. He took a swig from his flask and leaned back. "Don't know if I envy or pity you, friend. To limit yourself to one woman when there are countless of them, all with various skills and delights. What sort of prince doesn't desire more? You were born for greatness. For glory!"

Was I? It didn't seem that way. It seemed like I was born to be a monster, a harbinger of sorrow to revel in the shadow of my brother. Oh Brother Dearest, had the news reached his ears? Would he understand why? No. Of course not. The king was similar to our ruffian here in his ignorance of beauty. If Brother couldn't tell which women were perfect, he may as well have them all. "I was born to end lives. While my journey has led to many things, I assure you, greatness and glory are neither of them."

The ruffian rose with a sigh. "It's like talking to a rock. Here," he said, grabbing Dorothy and nudging her towards me. "Be a lass and entertain our prince. My advice? Keep him talking. My men are known to become violent when their ears stop working. Right now, silence holds a price I dare not pay."

"Don't leave me with this monster!" Dorothy screamed. She could not have done more damage to my heart if a blade had pierced it.

"Darling, please don't call me that," I said, trying to make my voice deeper. "Allow me an opportunity to explain myself. All of this, everything, I did it all for you." I eased my hand to hers. If only she could feel the gentle warmth of my touch, surely she would—

She slapped my hand away. "Monster! You killed him! You killed him in cold blood!"

I never understood that phrase. Blood is never cold. At least not when it flows out from a dagger wound. "Uncle was...*touching* you. Against your wishes! Against our wishes!"

Dorothy scoffed, which was odd, considering my words came from the heart. "The only thing I wish for is enough gold to feed my family. Prince or not, do not dare speak for me. Our relationship will never amount to more than business. Monster indeed. No wonder they couldn't put you on the throne."

Every word was blasphemy. Dorothy had a family? What family? I turned away from her and towards my hands, which were still covered in blood. Of course! It was shock. Shock and nothing more. Shock and nothing more...

Dorothy was yelling obscenities. Some of the words were so vile, I fear repeating them would make this tale unsellable on Rainforest, or whatever the soulless monopoly of your realm is called. I could take no more. I didn't want to feel. I didn't want to hear. To be quite honest, I didn't want to exist. All of my problems were overwhelming, but the Gift of Silence would immediately fix one of them. I leaned back, closed my eyes, and let the darkness—

I flinched as she grabbed me. "Are you mad? They will butcher us both! No...of course not. They will only kill you while I suffer the consequences. Lord Mute, if you truly hold any feelings for me, save your base desires, do not call upon the silence. I beg of you."

Several things came—feelings first, thoughts second. Hearts always work faster than the mind. "Oh Darling, if sound is the price of your love, then let the heavens scream our names." Behind my mask was the grandest of smiles. The ruffian—whatever his name was—had been correct: I was destined for greatness. For glory! I patiently waited for Dorothy to rest her head upon my shoulder.

I patiently waited, though it never occurred.

CHAPTER 3

Apathy Is A Terrible Judgment

fter thirty years of royalty, fallen prince or not, it was odd to awake in a prison cell. For all our cultural differences, the king of Ganfren apparently shared my brother's dislike for vagrants, for there were many of them, in various shapes, colors, and sizes. Prisons contain one of the sadder of truths: the quickest way to make everyone equal is to make them worthless.

Throughout the night, they had barraged me with slurs—most of which did not apply to my ethnicity or orientation but, nonetheless, were very offensive. Shockingly, my captors never removed my mask. Perhaps they feared what monstrous face lay beneath. Or perhaps they simply feared it would kill me and deprive them of their gold.

"Rise!" a guard said.

So I did, despite the pain in my legs, and despite the pain everywhere above my legs. To speak plainly, I was rather tired from all the beatings. It was beneath me to obey commands from a foreign jailor, but I would sing and perform a Balewind jig if it meant no more pain. Oh, what I would do to feel no more pain…

"The king demands your presence."

"May I wash first? I have had quite the evening. Or evenings,

I should say. Odd, how time continues to flow long after we stop perceiving it."

"Perhaps I was not clear, *Prince*. You are summoned, and you are summoned at once." Of all the terrible things I had been called in the past forty-eight or so hours, Prince was by far the most frustrating. I would never become king. Brother Dearest could drop dead from the plague and they would find someone else. Anyone else. Anyone without the taint of silence.

I flinched and scurried over as the guard crashed his stick into the prison bars. My quest to avoid beatings was not an honorable one, though it was one I walked well. "Upon weighing my options, I accept your king's proposal."

As the bars opened, there was a slight temptation to rush the man and let the dice fall as they may. That feeling quickly vanished when I noticed the broadsword on his right hip. Like most gambles, the most logical course of action would be to never play at all—

He stepped forward and slapped me across the side of my head, sending me down to one knee. How did he predict my defiance? Was he a mind reader? I braced for many things: another beating, another insult, another threat. I did not brace for him to grab my mask with both hands.

"*No!*" A desperate strength gave me the power to push him away and scurry to the corner of my cell. What kind of monster removes a man's mask? It was there for a reason! A mark for the realm to know I was cursed. If I had been born to anyone other than royalty, I would've "disappeared" and never been mentioned again. Some days, most nights, I welcomed such an alternative.

"What in the seven hells?" the guard said, gazing at me curiously. He seemed more surprised than angry, though I noticed his hand drift to his blade. "Listen, this can go one of two ways. Take the mask off yourself, or I remove it and whatever else with one clean swipe."

Could I defeat such a heavily-armored guard with no weapons and bruises and wounds all over my body? Probably not. It did not help that the man looked seasoned. That look. You know the one: shattered by the death of youth and unfulfilled promises. I would just be another nightmare in this man's dreams if I were to resist.

So, I didn't. I took a deep breath, trying—and failing—to calm my beating heart. At least Dorothy wasn't here. She had seen…parts of me, but never the face. She had asked once and I screamed at her. Our relationship had never been quite the same after that. Not sure why.

Oh, the guard was approaching. Fine. I clicked the latches in the back of my mask, then forced myself not to weep as it clanged upon the ground. I was naked. Not in the textbook definition, but in the way that all I desired to be hidden was now laid bare for the world to gawk at. I waited for gasps, screams, calamity, but nothing occurred. Perhaps my face was such an insult to the senses, no word or natural reaction would be appropriate.

"That's it?" the guard said, shaking his head as he got closer. "Suppose I owe Kendrick his two silver. Figured you were some fucking monster thing."

"I am a monster. You just haven't realized it yet." I don't think anyone remembers the exact moment when they accept they're not beautiful. Some struggle for decades, others learn rather quickly. For anyone still uncertain, I suggest making a joke about wielding uncompromising beauty. If your jest receives ire from the same sex, rejoice! For you are beautiful. If you receive laughs, well, the realm will always need more clowns. Several murmurs and whispers filled the air as I followed the guard out of my chambers. Odd that none of them screamed.

Ah, it was one of *those* kingdoms. Life above the cells was a grand life indeed. Chandeliers, tables, doors, all shimmering with shiny rocks whose names I never bothered to remember. I hate gemstones. They are worthless in every aspect other than visual appeal. Who decides what is beautiful and how? Rocks? Expensive, colorful rocks? At least the people here were staring and whispering. I didn't particularly enjoy being feared, but apathy is a terrible judgment. By the time a man realizes no one sees him, he is already gone.

"Halt," my escort said, grabbing my wrist with unnecessary strength. Why bother? Where could I possibly run off to? "When these doors open, slowly approach the middle of the throne room, then kneel when prompted. I have protected King Lector since he was a hump in his mother's belly. I shall not lose him. I shall never lose him." My escort spoke with such fire, though he probably had no idea that, like most guards, he was destined to be nothing more than a forgotten flame.

The doors opened. A loud bang followed as they crashed against the walls. A rather poor design, though I doubt our king desired unsolicited advice from a foreigner. I had seen these events in my own kingdom, so I slowly walked to the center of the room before my guard would nudge me. So many people. So many eyes. Did I mention how much I hated not wearing a mask?

"Halt, fair prince of Balewind," the king said as I reached the middle. "Do not kneel. You are my guest." Ah, I was his guest. What a grand honor.

The guards who had beaten me earlier must not have heard the announcement.

CHAPTER 4

SPIDERS

ne's state of mind can best be analyzed by their greatest fear. The happy fear the good times will eventually end, while the depressed expect their suffering to last forever. Oddly enough, King Lector Shaw didn't seem to fear anything. He stood in front of his crimson throne with perfect posture, while dirty-blonde hair draped down his red metal armor. By the pride on his face, one would think he had accomplished something noteworthy in the past thirty years.

I assumed it was my turn to speak, so I said, "Salutations, Your Majesty. Thank you for your generosity in welcoming me to Ganfren. May I take my leave?"

The king laughed and the room followed, which was odd, considering I did not jest. I wanted to return home. I wanted to go anywhere that wasn't here. Anywhere where the beatings did not follow. "Certainly, but hear me out first. I have words that may interest you. My only request? Resist the temptation to fill our court with silence. Forgive the lack of subtlety, but if at any moment my ears stop working, your neck will soon follow."

Everyone laughed, which was absurd, considering his threat was poorly worded. My neck would stop working? What did that even mean? "Lord king, I have no quarrel with you or your subjects. I just wish to return home."

"Home? And where would that be?"

There are few things more insufferable than foolish men trying to be clever. "Your Majesty, as you…as I'm sure you are aware, Dorothy and I reside in Balewind—quite happily, I may add. Tis true, I will likely hang for the murder of Uncle Gunther, but I accept my fate. Out of all my nightmares, all my regrets, his gruesome demise will never trouble me. He touched her. He *touched* her."

The king appeared confused until someone whispered in his ear. After a nod, he stared at me, grinning, like I was an entire feast of mutton and lamb. "You really don't know, do you? And here I thought you were an actor, some grand hero of theater. Your king brother has betrayed you, Lord Mute. Eleanor's brothel was meant to be your grave. Yet, as fate would have it, here you are, in a kingdom that is not your own, surrounded by those who wish you no harm whatsoever."

"Lord king, if we're going to stand here and lie to each other, be a gentleman and fetch us both a mask. Staring into untruthful eyes is no worse than the sun." Unfortunately, like most royalty, I spoke first and thought later. Betrayal? Why would Brother Dearest betray me? I was already his tool. There's no purpose for kings to murder pawns when they naturally drop dead on their own. Enough. I took a deep breath and asked the truly important question. "Where is Dorothy?"

"Safe."

I took a deeper breath, reminding myself he could read my facial expressions. While it was unlikely I would leave here alive, Dorothy had no reason to pay for my crimes. "Take my life if you must, but—"

"I find you fascinating," King Lector said, stepping down from his elevated throne and closer to me. "It's not every day a royal assassin stumbles into my realm. You must be quite efficient. Most in your profession die early enough to leave a pretty corpse."

"There are good assassins, and there are dead ones. Tis the law of the blade."

"Law of the blade," he said, studying me like I was a painting. "For someone a mere step away from oblivion, you speak rather calmly. It's difficult to threaten such a man. Death doesn't frighten you, does it? Does anything? Entertain a royal curiosity. What does Lord Mute fear?"

I nearly fell over in shock. What did I fear? How could anyone ask such a personal question? It would be no worse than a stranger asking about the queen's feet. If I had any sort of weapon, I would've killed the man where he stood. What did I fear? Well, here's a start: I feared the fact that at thirty-one years of age, I had not learned to be happy. It's easy to blame the Gift of Silence, but it goes deeper; deeper to a point where it's difficult to manifest into words. Happiness is a riddle I swear everyone has solved but me. And with every year that goes by, every blink from day to night, my time to figure it out slowly fades, like sand trickling down the hourglass.

"Spiders," I said.

"Of course." After an awkward pause, the king yelled, "Enough! This calls for a feast!" He raised his arms and rallied up the onlookers. Why was he…Oh, he was mad. I was usually better at spotting these things. Why do the mad ones always end up in power? Most would be better off writing terrible literature.

The crowd still cheered as their king stomped around like a fool. Was I supposed to do something? I just stood there, unsure of what to do with my hands. Honestly, I considered walking out until the king stared me dead in the eyes. It was not a pleasant look. He rushed over and grabbed me with more strength than expected. I was unsure if it was intentional, but the king's grip made it clear who would prevail if we came to blows.

"Prince Mute, my handmaiden shall provide escort to your own personal bath. I have a…let's call it premonition, that the two of us will be grand friends indeed."

I didn't want to be Lector's friend, though I didn't wish to die, so I nodded and said, "Of course, Your Grace." As if on cue, a pleasant-looking woman took me by the hand. Her age and demeanor reminded me of Beatrice from Eleanor's. Oh, how I missed those days. Never a good sign to be nostalgic for the "better days" of last week.

"Lord Mute," she said, caressing my palm with one finger. If she meant the move as a seduction method, it was uncomfortable and I wished she would stop. "Time to freshen up! How do you feel about…*lavender?*"

"Splendid choice. Lead the way, Love." Honestly, I would've said yes to anything. While the quality of most scents are subjective, I could scarcely name one worse than my current scenario.

It was a slow walk to the bathing area. Our journey took us to a lower level of the castle. For a moment, I assumed it was all lies and I was being led back to a prison cell. She continued that strange finger gesture the entire time. I probably could've told her to stop, but I didn't want to make things awkward, which of course, made things more awkward.

Fortunately, the bathing area was well-kept. It took a moment to realize mine was on the other side of the room, an isolated corner hidden by curtains. As we drifted forward, my eyes failed to resist the temptation of watching people relax in their baths. Unlike home, the baths here were pure anarchy. Men and women bathed in unison, completely in the nude, gesturing and chatting like such debauchery was completely normal. Where was the decency? I held back a rather judgmental scoff. Nudity is never something to flaunt.

We finally reached the private bathing area. I stood by the edge of the water, silently waiting for my escort to leave. I silently waited for quite a while.

"Lord Mute," she finally said. "Do you require…some sort of assistance?"

"Privacy. Is such a thing unheard of in Ganfren?"

"Goodness," she said with a giggle—one that reminded me of Dorothy. "I have seen all sorts of men, in all sorts of shapes and sizes. You have nothing to fear, my lord. No woman earns her wrinkles without learning how to keep a secret."

I grinned at her for being so foolish. "Well, if we are surrendering our subtlety, allow me to be blunt. The only ones allowed to see me in such a state are my mother and future wife. My mother is dearly departed, and last I checked, we are not betrothed."

To my surprise, she met my grin with her own as she approached and took my coat. "Blunt, you say? How blunt, Lord Mute? Rest assured, I want no part of you. But such a choice is no longer my own. Like you, I am an actor. My hair is gray, and my heart is dark. Now take off your damn clothes."

I obliged. This woman clearly wore scars my eyes could not see. As my clothes fell softly to the ground, it was both a relief and disappointment to notice the utter apathy in her eyes. I was nothing to her and, like most of my encounters in this state, it only left me feeling empty.

I wasn't sure how they kept the water so warm. I caught no glimpse of fire, and even these heathens would not dare use magic in the open. Easing my feet into the water felt wonderful. Easing everything else was not. To be fair, it was some odd mixture of ecstasy and agony. The wounds burned but the flesh welcomed the warmth. I slid down to my neck, resisting the temptation to sink to the bottom and never rise again.

Quite some time had passed as I closed my eyes and pondered better days. A young brother. A loving mother. A dead father. Baths are truly underrated. I could have stayed there forever.

"Time to rise, Lord Mute."

CHAPTER 5

You Ruined My Life

As I buttoned the last button of my fancy shirt within my "guest" chambers, I couldn't help but meet eyes with the stranger in the mirror. Time never fails to reveal how ugly our choices have made us. At least King Lector had returned my mask. I put it back so my reflection would appear more familiar.

A knock came at the door. I had no choice but to assume it was a coincidence that it came mere moments after I finished dressing. "Enter," I said, purely by instinct. Of course they would enter. I nearly forgot I was their prisoner, draped in expensive and uncomfortable garments.

"Good evening, Lord Mute." It was the older lady from earlier. At some point, I should've asked her name. "Ah! You look rather stunning!" she said, with enough sarcasm to cure the plague. "Before we begin, enlighten me. What do you know of King Lector Shaw?"

"Enough."

She stared at me, clearly expecting more. I didn't want to tell this woman her king was a fool, though, to be fair, she probably already knew. She approached and tugged my collar. "My lord, our fates are intertwined. Don't fuck this up." The spite in her voice made me yearn for Beatrice. In hindsight, while women stuck with the worst of men do in fact become the best of actors, they eventually grow tired. Very tired.

"Thank you for being openly rude, my lady. It's refreshing."

She sighed, took my arm, and nudged me out of my chambers. It seemed like the perfect opportunity to finally inquire her name—

"Dorothy?" My heart and feet stopped in unison. She stood outside the doorway in a dazzling blue dress, an azure joining of the sky and however we remember the ocean from our happier days. I held back the temptation to embrace her. While she couldn't see my smile, the horrified scowl on her face was impossible to ignore. "Does my mere presence make you suffer? Must you loathe me with such uncompromising ire?"

"You ruined my life." It took only four words to destroy me. Thank each one of the vile gods she couldn't see my face. I did not weep. Not out of defiance, but from the mere desperation to maintain my pride. How could she speak with such venom? Of course! It was shock. Shock and nothing more…

"Even you must understand we're both going to die here. I can only pray my son will persevere without me. The boy is too young to struggle through this realm alone."

Her what?

"What did you say? What did you just say?" By pure instinct, I grabbed her arm and ignored her gasp. "We have a child? A *son*?" I could hardly contain myself. The missing piece of my life had been there all along! "His name…tell me his name!" Even I was realistic enough not to expect a Mute Jr or anything of the sort, but I couldn't care less. I had a child! A boy!

Why did the question horrify her? She started to say something until the older woman did a not-so-subtle cough. But why? The child was obviously mine. Who else would dare touch Dorothy? Uncle had tried and paid the price, screaming silently as blood poured down his neck. The two women were looking at each other, making strange mouth gestures. I hate these sort of things. Did they prefer silence? I could arrange that.

"If we survive our time here, I will introduce you to the boy. He has…I think…you will favor him."

Well of course I would favor him. Other than my own father, what father doesn't favor their own son? "I assure you, Darling, you will survive, or this kingdom shall suffer a requiem of silence." Obviously, it was unwise to make such an outlandish threat in front of Not-Beatrice, but so be it. Happiness finally became more than a dream. It was one of those things that could not be seen or touched, but felt within my silent heart. I would teach the boy how to navigate this cruel world. I would teach him the proper respect, manners, when to use a large word and when to bring your vocabulary down to the level of fools. Most importantly…

I would teach him to be nothing like me.

"Come. The king awaits," said my escort, taking me by the arm and nudging me forward through the hallway. To be quite honest, I was unimpressed with my surroundings. All the portraits were dusty, the carpets were wet and discolored for some reason, and ugh, the green and yellow gemstones didn't mesh with the red themes at all. I nearly wished Brother Dearest would conquer this kingdom, if only to introduce an interior decorator.

"Why does the king desire our presence?" asked Dorothy. A fair question. I probably should have asked first but was too distracted by my son awaiting me back home. Who cares what the king wants? Name your request. Done. Granted. I would fulfill his outrageous demands and make up for lost time. How old was my boy? Oh! I still hadn't caught his name.

"Girl, I wish I knew. With King Lector, the request could be anything. I hope it goes without saying that you must obey. I'm not worried about you, of course, but our prince here…"

"Our prince here what?" I said, with a tad more anger than

intended. Just because I wore a mask, it didn't give them an excuse to pretend I didn't see the realm for how it was. "I have spent my entire life fulfilling the demands of royalty. What is one more rock upon a mountain of service?"

Not-Beatrice opened the doors without an apology—which was very rude.

My mask hid my cocked eyebrow as we entered the empty throne room. Naturally, I assumed the meeting would take place in front of a crowd. What better opportunity for a king craving attention to flaunt his new toy?

Each step through the halls created a tiny echo. How annoying that we didn't walk in unison. Our journey was an off-tempo cacophony, haunted by lonely seats flanking us on both sides. I always avoided my own throne room back home when it was empty. Not out of superstition or any childish notions, but out of the premonition that an empty throne room is a prelude to a dead kingdom.

Behind the throne was a doorway I hadn't noticed during my first visit. Not-Beatrice slowly approached and tapped three times. After an uncomfortable pause, the king's voice called out, "You may enter."

So we did. I was surprised—and quite impressed—with the king's quaint little study. None of the opulence of gems and diamonds could be found, instead, replaced by a desk, a round table, and a crackling fireplace. A bookcase was on the left, filled with tomes of history and philosophy. Unsurprisingly, the perfect spines suggested the books had never been opened. There are few things more tragic than a book in flawless condition.

The king cracked his knuckles as he rose from his desk. He smiled at me—somehow staring straight into my eyes—and took a seat at his table. There were only three remaining seats available, so I wasn't sure why he gestured to them as if we had any choice. "Tell me, assassin, how are you enjoying your accommodations thus far?"

For all the people I had slain over the years, it was odd how rarely anyone referred to me as assassin or even murderer. I always assumed it was out of fear. No one refers to a monster as a monster to their face unless they're looking for trouble and, hopefully, this king wasn't looking for trouble. I had far more important concerns awaiting back home. "I am quite satisfied. My friend here has been a gracious host. All things considered."

"And you, Dorothy? Don't think for a moment I forgot about you." I did not appreciate the king's glare. It was filled with many things, subtlety not being one of them.

"I am eternally grateful for your kindness and hospitality," said Dorothy, in the tone of true royalty. Perhaps, in a better realm, she could have been the queen for King Mute...

"Good. Lord Mute, I have given you time, and I can only pray you haven't been wasteful. Have you come to terms with your brother's betrayal? If so, it will make the remainder of this conversation much, much easier."

This madness again? Fine. Brother Dearest would never betray me, but if my journey to happiness was mapped on a path of lies, I would gladly follow. "Reality does not require validation. The truth shall set me free."

"Right," the king said, taking a sip from his chalice. Even from across the table I could smell the wine, though the scent was more likely coming from his skin than his chalice. "In that case, I must ask: how does your brother's betrayal make you feel?"

Foolish questions often deserve foolish answers, but there was too much at stake. I resisted the temptation for a dramatic lie. Despite the mask, theater had never been my strong point. It's always easier to blend truth and lies. For whatever reason, the two flow quite naturally. "Of all the words available, wounded would be most precise. I have experienced many wounds in the past two weeks, Your Grace."

"Wounds are just scars in denial." The king leaned back as if he had just said something profound. He had not. "Let me ask my question another way. How would you feel if your brother were to…let's say…no longer be king?"

I could only hope he didn't notice me flinch, though I likely hoped in vain. "I would weep, of course. How else should one act during a tragedy?"

"Mute, please," said Dorothy.

The king raised a hand to silence her. "No, no. It's okay. Perhaps I expected too much. With the way you…handled your uncle, I was led to believe my offer would be more intriguing."

"I never heard any offer," I said, keeping my mask straight but glancing around the room. "Unless…Truly? How could you ask me to perform such a dreadful task? Fool or not, the man is my brother." My finger tapped the table. While I hated the sound, my body moved by itself. Too many emotions were coming out to control any of them.

"Think, Mute! Think! Did that evening ever strike you as odd? An anonymous letter warned us well in advance of the plot. We had enough forces in that room to squash a militia." He laughed then said, "Archibald wasn't even in the brothel. He wasn't anywhere near Balewind. I have the exact wording from the letter itself." Lector cleared his throat then said, "'Unfortunately, my brother's madness has poisoned him to his very core. I suspect the Silent God's influence has finally pulled him below the point of no return. Mute has confessed his sinister plot to slay Emissary Archibald during his next visit. In the name of mutual cooperation, and open tradelines, slay the mad prince with extreme prejudice. You have my blessing.' Here," Lector said, handing a paper to Not-Beatrice, who then handed it to me.

I knew the words would be there before I read them. I stopped after the first sentence, then my eyes lingered on the royal seal at the bottom. "Why am I still alive?" My question was spoken to the king, but I meant it for the world itself. Why was I still here? There had been so many opportunities in my life to either die or achieve greatness, and yet, all I did was linger on, flowing with the tide of mediocrity.

The king rose. "Because you are more than a tool. You are more than a blade. You are more than the silence that curses you. I saw it in your eyes the very first time we met. Your destiny awaits…King Mute."

King Mute? Interesting. I always wanted to be king, though I'm not sure why. I had no taxation policy, no real aptitude for military games, and I found treaties and geopolitical conflicts rather boring. I could love and I could kill. That seemed to summarize my entire thirty-one years. My only saving grace was a lack of madness.

Thank the gods for that.

The king continued speaking but my attention was elsewhere. "I'll do it," I said, interrupting him mid-sentence. "But on one condition. Dorothy will be my queen."

"Done. I assumed as much. Take the girl with you. I prepared all sorts of treaties and documents, all signed, all bearing my crest. Show them to your brother, then show him your dagger. Stay here a few weeks, then we set our plan into motion. Any questions?"

Dorothy's face was a bright red. She looked like she wanted to speak but her words would have to wait. This was a conversation between kings.

I was unsure why this man desired my ascension and I couldn't care less. "All cloak and dagger aside, will the two of us remain allies? I must admit, my days here have been surprisingly pleasant. When the time comes, it would be nice to have a friend."

The king smiled. "Consider me a friend for life…Your Majesty."

What an eventful day. I had a son and, soon, I would have a kingdom.

CHAPTER 6

ORION

could not recall waking up, but there I was, standing in the middle of the Balewind throne room. I could not recall making the journey, and I definitely could not recall ousting my brother as king. Fresh blood dripped down the dagger in my right hand. Oh, of course: a dream. I tried to wake myself but to no avail. Dreams were rather annoying but at least they weren't nightmares. I stopped having those when my mind had given up trying to conjure scenarios worse than reality.

"Hello, Deary," a voice echoed from behind.

When people think of queens, they tend to think of royalty or power. I immediately thought of my mother. I had lost her at far too young an age. In many ways, it was the wound that scarred me forever. Mother had no portraits, no memorabilia; she was just the loving woman from my memories. Her appearance was slightly different each time I dreamed. Eventually, she would become an unrecognizable tapestry of sorrow. Perhaps that had already occurred. Perhaps the woman in front of me was so far removed from reality, no one would recognize her but me.

"Hello, Mother. Fancy seeing you here."

"Where else would I be?" she said with a smile. "And why the blade? You are home. No need for weapons here. You boys never listen."

I held the dagger out in front of me. My face reflected in the steel; for whatever reason, my mask never followed into my dreams. "Sorry Mother but the blade is a necessary evil. The time has come to reclaim what is mine by birthright."

Her dismissive laughter hurt me like it always did. "'Mine' is a rather dangerous word, Deary. You are beginning to sound like your father. And your brother. Imagine that."

"With a snap of my fingers, I don't have to sound like anyone."

"How predictable. All the men in my life unleash their anger in such interesting ways. Father with his fist, Merrick with his paranoia, and you with your silence. You can hide from reality for a time, but no one escapes it forever."

I sheathed the dagger in my belt, uncaring if the blood stained my garments. In a few moments, none of this would exist, anyway. "I never chose the life of a murderer. I should have been king."

Mother approached with a smile, and I couldn't help but step back. Despite her tiny size, she may as well have been an ogre from the South. "No, my son. You were never meant to be king. And you were certainly never meant to be a murderer. Oh, the cost of our family's sins are indeed vast. They love you in their own way. They just don't understand you."

"And you do? Or did, I should say?"

"I understand my boy is in pain. The rest doesn't matter. Orion, abandon this mad task. Such a path will only trade one nightmare for another. I raised you, and I know you better than anyone or anything in this realm. You are a good boy. The burden of a fallen brother will melt away whatever lingers of your humanity."

"Don't call me Orion," I said, turning away. No one had called me that name since…Mother had died. Orion had laughed.

Orion had played in the gardens with Brother. Orion had been beaten and forced to wear a mask for being born with a power he never understood. Now, I was Mute and nothing more. Mute…and nothing more.

Mother grabbed my neck and lifted me high above the ground. I swore she grew several feet larger, and her eyes grew wide as fangs materialized in her mouth. "I can live with you forgetting your own mother's face, but do not *ever* forget your true name. This world is filled with terrors and madness—most of which I have no power to protect you from. I shall say it again: abandon this mad task. Abandon your harlot. It's long past time that you made your own purpose in this life. If you keep allowing the realm to treat you as a weapon, that's all you'll ever be."

I collapsed to the ground as her grip loosened. "I have always been a weapon. If I can admit the truth, so can you." I glanced upwards to watch her disapproval, but she was nowhere to be found. I was alone, curled up on the ground, seeping in the endless amount of blood flowing out of my dagger. "Wait. Come back. Mother…come back. Don't leave me in this world alone. Please…"

With a gasp, reality woke me from my slumber. My heart pounded, my breath was short, and I immediately clutched my mask to make sure it was still there. It took a moment to compose myself. What a bizarre dream. I was unsure why my mind felt it necessary to barrage me with such madness. To worship the past means giving up on the future. But…Mother was gone. For all my troubled memories, that one would never fade. Her funeral still felt like yesterday. A black veil had covered her face as they lowered her grave into the soil.

I hadn't realized it until much later, but as she made her decent, all my dreams of ever being happy followed.

CHAPTER 7

HAVEN'T FELT THE COLD IN YEARS

 took a large gulp of water. Not out of thirst, but I needed to feel any sort of relief after last night's dream. With the euphoria of bravado gone, I glanced into the mirror and let the questions flow. Was my newfound "friend" trustworthy? Would Dorothy accept her role as queen? If Brother Dearest had truly conspired against me, what would stop him from executing me the moment I arrived back home? Could my son love a king-slayer? If not, could I force him to?

A bath would have been nice, but I had a feeling it was best to leave here as soon as possible. My bags were ready, my mask was secure and, for the time being, my dagger was clean. I opened the door, disappointed Not-Beatrice wasn't there to greet me. A pity to have never learned her name. With packed bags across my shoulder, I slowly walked through the halls, perhaps for the final time. King Lector had called me a friend, but with no one here to offer their farewell, it didn't feel like I had any friends at all.

Perhaps in a different life, I could have learned to love Ganfren. The gemstones weren't all that bad after a few weeks. They shimmered their silly colors, flaunting a wealth unknown to the common folk outside the castle. If there was anything both our kingdoms excelled at, it was ensuring the poor dreamed of wealth but never achieved it.

"Lord Mute?" Dorothy's voice! I immediately turned and grinned, though she couldn't see it. "I was nervous when your quarters were empty. It would be most wise to stick together during our departure. I have a suspicious feeling that nothing is as it seems."

"Darling, take your suspicions and bury them next to your old life. A wonderful, royal destiny awaits us both."

"You aren't afraid, my prince? Not even a tad nervous? Doesn't our fortune seem too good to be true?"

I took her by the hand. To my delight, she did not flinch or deny me. "Nothing is too good for kings. But don't take my word for it. Come, allow me to show you." With Dorothy on my arm, I quickened my pace through the halls, eager to leave this kingdom and find my son. Still, I had to be realistic. The boy would not favor me at first. I would be seen as a stranger, as an odd-looking fellow who had done things to his mother he would not understand until he grew older.

I paused as we stepped outside the castle doors for two reasons. One, a rare sense of good fortune. I had come here as a prisoner, as a dead man, and left with a queen on my arm and a dagger by my side. Two, because King Lector had already arrived, surrounded by soldiers and scholarly-looking people. White robes, poorly groomed beards, sandals. You know the type.

"Lord Mute!" Lector called out, noticing me immediately. How the man was always able to stare directly into my eyes was concerning. "Take this," he said, handing me a bag filled with papers and documents I did not recognize. "I put the primary treaty up top. It authorizes the Dilfoy Tradelines for both parties. It's the one that nearly cost your life. Offer Merrick that agreement first to gain his trust. The next part…well, I'll leave that to you. Forgive the unsolicited advice, but my only suggestion is to make it quick. Don't let him speak. The voice of a dead brother lingers for a long time. A *very* long time." Hmm. I honestly wished he hadn't said that. The official story had been that Lector's older brother had fallen in battle. Perhaps that part was true, but who he had fallen against was certainly debatable.

"I shall carry your warning in my heart. Your Majesty, before I take my leave, please accept my gratitude for everything. May our friendship be a prelude to peace and prosperity for both kingdoms."

The king's sudden embrace caught me by surprise. It was one of the few times I could recall anyone hugging me without first receiving gold. After a pause, I returned his embrace. It was nice to hold someone, and even nicer to be held. Part of me wished my family would have hugged me more often. Or anyone.

Oh well, no time for such thoughts.

"I'll send an ambassador when news reaches this side of the realm. In about six months, maybe a year, two at most, we shall have a summit of kings. There, we can finally combine our forces and reclaim the South. Those heathens and their witchcraft shall insult the natural order of things no longer. I hear they even dare speak the Silent God's name out loud. Every last one of them will beg for their end long before I hand it to them."

To be honest, I had no idea what he was referring to. I never had any issues with the South. I would never admit such a thing out loud, but their open acceptance of magic seemed rather pleasant, though speaking the Silent God's name out loud was… questionable. Imagine that: a life where I wouldn't be a monster. A life without a mask. "I eagerly await our reunion. Our enemies shall tremble before our combined might."

"Indeed they shall." The king snapped his fingers at a familiar-looking fellow, who jumped to attention and rushed over. "My friend here will be your guide back to Balewind. I understand you may have reservations after…well, you know, but I trust this man wholeheartedly. He is not a good man. He is certainly not a wise man. But he is a man who loves gold. When you become king, surround yourself with them."

"Indeed," I said, hoping the distrust didn't linger in my voice. I didn't want this man anywhere near me or my Dorothy. Whatever his name was. For now, Uneducated Ruffian would have to suffice.

Uneducated Ruffian hugged me. Two hugs in one day, what a miracle. "You have made me a wealthy, wealthy man," he said, showing that awful, toothless grin as he released me. "And look! Your lady friend! I dare say she looks delicious, my lord."

"Mind your tongue in front of the future queen," I said, as Dorothy stepped behind me. While the two of us never had much in common, at least we both found this man detestable. The thrill of the moment made me approach him and stand face-to-face. "It would seem our roles have reversed, sir. From henceforth, you work for me. Never forget that."

"Sure thing, Brother," he said, patting me on the shoulder as he jumped into the cart. Why didn't the man fear me? Perhaps he was unaware of my reputation, or was too uneducated to understand the proper dynamics of fear. "Keep making me that gold and we can perform any roles you want. At this rate, even my bastards will own land. Well, if you're all set, you may as well hop in. We should avoid the snow if we leave immediately."

Leaving immediately would be most convenient. I stepped into the cart first, then took Dorothy by the hand and pulled her in. I used more strength than necessary in hopes of impressing her, though she didn't seem to notice.

It was a bit cramped for royalty, and the smell was unfortunate. Very unfortunate. I couldn't tell if it was from the animals pulling the cart, or the animals already drinking wine hours before sun fall. It was nearly enough to make me laugh. Addicts, thieves, murderers, all sporting golden rings but missing most of their teeth. At least Dorothy stayed close. I assumed she still saw me as a monster, but perhaps better the monster you know or however the phrase goes.

"Last call!" Uneducated Ruffian yelled. To my dismay, three more men leaped into the cart. Then, after a crack of the whip, the horses started running.

I noticed Dorothy shiver. Perhaps because I kept staring at her. "A touch of cold, Darling?"

"I can manage."

"Nonsense. Take my coat," I said, handing it to her. While I would have preferred to lean on each other and let body warmth perform the job, courting my queen would be a war of tiny victories. "Save your objections. I will entertain none of them."

Dorothy accepted my offer after a pause. She pulled the coat close and wrapped it around her body. "Very well. Thank you, Lord Mute. Are you not cold yourself?"

I smiled, though she wouldn't see it through my mask. "Funny you should ask. I haven't felt the cold in years."

CHAPTER 8

THE SILENT GOD

The first day of travel had been very boring. I will do you a courtesy and omit several pages of us sitting in a cart doing nothing. By early afternoon, day two was looking to be around the same. Still, I was smart enough not to complain. Boring trips don't make for great stories, but most catastrophes are tales that never get told. Wait, why were we slowing down?

"Why are we slowing down?" I asked, attempting to sound as regal as possible. If yesterday had been an example for the rest of the trip, we still had several hours before the next break.

"Shut up," said Uneducated Ruffian. "Everyone shut up for a moment."

"We're being robbed," Dorothy whispered. "Have you a spare weapon?"

"Queens wield scepters, not blades. Fear not, Darling, the dagger on my hip is worth an entire army." I wasn't sure how true any of those words were, so I made sure to speak them with the utmost confidence.

We came to a complete stop.

"And what do we have here?" said a different uneducated fellow. From what I could see through the small gap at the front of the cart, he appeared to be heavily armed. "You weren't planning on passing on by without paying the toll, were you now?"

"Brother, I am on a task commissioned by King Lector Shaw himself. I don't care who you rob in these parts. But don't rob me."

I sighed, for our brilliant escort may as well had proclaimed we were overflowing with gold. My right hand went to my dagger. I took a deep breath to stop the shaking. This wasn't like a standard assassination. The art of violence is most effective when only one party knows the violence is about to occur.

"Oh? You hear that, lads? Commissioned by King Lector Shaw!" The thief laughed, then yelled, "Oh glorious king! King of kings! If our actions betray the throne, let Lepock himself drown me in silence." Along with being thieves, these men were clearly heathens—and more likely insane. To even whisper the Silent God's name was grounds for execution in any civilized kingdom. And grounds for other fates, far, far worse.

"Seven hells!" Uneducated Ruffian yelled. "*Never* speak his name. Are you mad?"

"Lepock, Lepock, Lepock—"

"Listen you fucking *heathen*, I have eight men willing to protect this cart with their lives. Our forces look about equal by my count. If you feel the need to roll the dice and damn yourself more than you already have, be my guest and make the first move."

And of course, Uneducated Ruffian was slain immediately after those words, leaving the rest of us in a very unfortunate scenario. To my surprise, our men rushed out from the cart, all screaming, all raising their weapons high in the air. I admired their confidence, though I could have done without the screaming. It certainly didn't help that Dorothy screamed as well. For all her beauty, for all her perfection, her scream was awful. The high-pitched wail was like a blade through my ears. Between my queen and the battle, I could take no more.

I closed my eyes, cleared my mind, and focused on nothing. "*Hush*," I whispered, then the forest went deaf.

Ah, much better. I rose from my corner of the cart and stretched my arms. I waved one finger at Dorothy, hoping she would comprehend it meant, "One moment, Darling." I held back a silent laugh as I stepped outside. While most of the men still fought, others ran in a panic through the woods, all clutching their ears. Rather annoying that both sides wore black. Still, I could identify my allies…for the most part.

One of the thieves was searching through the pockets of our fallen Uneducated Ruffian. In hindsight, that name was unworthy of my guide. Henceforth, my old friend was simply Ruffian. I slowly approached the thief. What a strange man. He was so utterly obsessed with thievery, he didn't even spare me a glance as I closed the distance. Men like this didn't deserve sound. Not sight, smell, nor taste.

I left out touch for a reason.

My blade pierced the side of his neck instead of tearing straight through the middle. It would slay him eventually, but I wanted him to suffer for as long as possible. His eyes went wide as blood poured out from the wound. I pushed him to the ground and casually approached two thieves who were clubbing one of my allies. Out of all the weapons, out of all the means to kill a man, clubs were such a bizarre choice. Even an axe or halberd would've been more dignified.

I slit the first man's throat and waited for his friend to react in desperation. He did—though he swung at my ribs and not my mask. An odd move, though effective. I lunged forward with my dagger. We exchanged blows, and all the air fled my body as the club bashed its designated target. With the Gift of Silence still active, I screamed as loud as I could, which was not loud at all. I tore my blade out of his neck and stumbled back, fell to one knee, and tried to control my breathing.

It was rather concerning that my vision started to fade. Perhaps becoming king was not my destiny. Perhaps my destiny was to die in the middle of…wherever this was, slain by a club. I fell to the ground, stared into the sky, and saw something I had only seen one other time in my life.

I can hear my name from worlds apart, yet I hear nothing at all. I have missed you, Orion. My silent little prince. You have grown so much, yet not at all. Off to play king, are we? I would favor that. A silent crown for a silent kingdom.

Every word from Lepock—God of Silence—was a force within my skull. Not exactly a scream, but more a deafening whisper. "Leave me alone," I said, and I'm still unsure if he heard me. "I never wanted this. I never—"

Dorothy grabbed my mask and tried to scream at me. She didn't seem to understand how this whole "forest went deaf" thing worked. At least the sight of my queen sent the blurriness away. That was enough shame for one day. I grabbed my dagger and forced myself up. I had a role to play. Not for Lector, not for Lepock, not even for Dorothy.

For Lord Mute, the Silent King.

I stabbed some other guy. Honestly, I think he was already dead, but I wanted to look powerful in front of my queen. I ensured my eyes didn't linger on the sky as I rushed the next man. Anything to avoid Lepock. What a cruel world, where I could not recall my mother's face, but the Silent God's single eye and black wings were engraved into my very essence. It would most likely be the final thing I saw before my demise.

I gripped the other man's leather armor as I slammed my dagger into his chest, over and over, trying to find any sort of relief from his suffering. None was found. I had received the Silent God's gift as a child. Even back then, beatings had been commonplace, but the closed-fisted punch to the face when my father had first heard me say "Lepock" was an unforgettable pain.

The man in my arms was quite dead. He had probably died from the first stab; fear always makes blades grow sharper. I released him, took a deep breath, and leaned against a tree. That was enough. I couldn't recall the exact number, but I had slain at least five of them. My forces would have to finish the rest.

I resisted the temptation to rest my eyes when I noticed Dorothy staring into the sky, seemingly frozen. Ah, that look of terror and denial. I knew she would rush off long before she actually did. It was written on her legs and on her face. Part of me was okay with that—but not the heart.

And the heart always wins.

CHAPTER 9

WHAT ARE YOU?

peed had never been my strong point, but I dashed through the forest as quickly as my legs would allow. It was rather awkward without sound. I leaned on my eyesight to avoid tripping on some overgrown tree branch or wildlife. Up ahead, Dorothy was a flicker in my vision. She ran like she had seen the edge of oblivion. If my suspicions were correct, she probably had.

Thank the gods she was slowing down. Dorothy's legs gave out as she fell to her knees and vomited on the soil. While it was unpleasant to observe, I wouldn't hold it against her.

"He's real!" she yelled. The words were silent but I could usually follow lips. "All those warnings. All those tales. They were real." She stopped looking at the soil and, for the first time I could remember, she stared directly into my eyes. "What are you?"

What a rude question. You can't just ask people what they are. Bold of her to assume I had any idea. All my life I had been Mute and nothing more. Whatever that meant. I considered trying to answer her question, but with my mask still on, she wouldn't have been able to read my lips.

I took a gamble and reached out my hand. Her options were quite limited, but those in fear tend to act first and think later. To my delight, she took my hand and allowed me to pull her up. It was one of the only times in my life I wished sound was available. I had so much I wanted to say, so many questions I wanted to answer. It took a moment to realize my hand was shaking as she held it. I always hated fear, despite how naturally it came to me.

We must go back, I thought, but could not say. All I could do was keep a loose grip and leave towards the way we came. Oh, how I wished to hold her dearly. To tighten my grip, to grab Dorothy and ensure she never ran away again. Instead, I kept walking. It was nice in a way. Despite all the madness unleashed upon us in the past few days, all we had to do was walk. We walked and walked and walked and walked…

Sorry, I know this part isn't very interesting. Before you leave a scathing review on Pleasant Reads—or whatever the largest book community, which happens to be owned by the largest soulless monopoly of your realm, is called—I'll skip ahead.

However much time later, we arrived back at the cart. Apparently, my men had been victorious. Ruffian was still slain, though if I knew anything about these sorts, another Uneducated Ruffian had already taken his place. Still, I would miss the man. There was something about his…passion that was admirable.

"I never learned his name," I said. It took a moment to realize the words were spoken out loud. For better or for worse, sound had returned to the forest.

"Eh, it happens," a man said, wiping blood off his own tunic. "On a cheery note, his loss is our gain. More gold with less people means rich men indeed." If King Lector was anything like my brother, they wouldn't receive any additional reward, save for an unmarked grave. "We should really get moving. I feel a chill in the air. Those savage bastards spoke the Silent God's name out loud. Never heard such blasphemy."

"Lepock," Dorothy said.

I nearly fell over. To hear my future wife speak of such evil was outrageous. "Enough!" I yelled, trying to sound like a monster. For whatever reason, the tone came quite naturally. "The battle has concluded. We achieved victory, but at great cost. Now, the journey must continue." I really wasn't sure what else to say. I was never prone to thanking people for doing their job.

One of the advantages of grouping with ruffians was no one felt the need to bury the dead. Tragic as it may have been, it saved us a lot of time. Still, I couldn't help but stare at the bodies as they slowly faded out of view. What a meaningless end. Had it truly all been for gold? Seemed rather sad to dedicate an entire existence to hoarding a currency that meant nothing in the afterlife. Perhaps my life as a prince had made me blind to such struggles. Try as I may, it was difficult to understand, and even more so to care.

"You never answered my question," said Dorothy, who sat farther away from me.

"And which one would that be?" I knew of course, but I wanted her to say it out loud. I wanted her to feel the shame of wounding me.

She shifted just a tiny bit closer. "What are you?"

"Quite simple. I am Mute and nothing more. Satisfied?"

"No!" she yelled which, unfortunately, drew several eyes towards us. "If our fates are interwoven, I need to understand what…who I'm dealing with."

I sighed. If she wanted to be cruel, I would oblige—and most likely regret it later. "You speak out of fear, which tends to cast a wide web, yet traps nothing but pain and regret. What am I, you ask? What is my purpose? Darling, I have no idea. I couldn't guess even if you put a knife to my throat. Now if you would, please stop wounding me. My broken ribs offer more than enough ache for one trip."

It was no surprise when she got up to sit at the farthest end of the cart. To be honest, I welcomed the solitude. I couldn't recall exactly when it had occurred, but I had lost count of all the men who had died by my dagger long before today's escapade. I had tried to keep even a conservative estimate, but math isn't open to interpretation. It's harrowing to realize you cannot atone for your sins when there are too many to remember.

No one seemed to care what sort of toll that takes on a man.

CHAPTER 10

DENIAL

f day one of our journey had been uneventful, days three, four, and five were even more so. I held high hopes for day six, for it was the first time I could make sense of where we were. The outskirts of Balewind.

Home.

The whimsical feeling of being reunited with my brother was drowned by the reality of what our reunion meant. It occurred to me I hadn't thought of it much during my journey. For all my strengths, my ability to ignore reality was rather powerful. Could I really do it? Easily in the physical sense—it doesn't take much effort for a blade to end a life. But mentally? Emotionally? Whatever you may believe, I still loved my brother. The two of us were the only remaining fragments of the Elmere Dynasty. Five generations of royalty could all come crashing down, annihilated by the cursed prince unfit to be king.

"We're home," Dorothy said, sadly enough, without a smile. I could only wonder what thoughts swam through her pretty little head. I had no choice but to wonder, because she wouldn't tell me. We hadn't spoken much in the past few days. It was a natural silence, unlike the ones created with a whisper. "What happens now?"

My future queen seemed driven to ask unanswerable questions. As I struggled to find the words, it seemed rather clear this whole ordeal had been poorly planned. "One of two scenarios. If Brother Dearest believes my tale, I will return to the castle and…figure out the next step. If Brother Dearest correctly believes I am a liar, well, my journey shall reach its conclusion. Whatever occurs, do not follow me to the grave. I can accept my own demise, but our son needs a mother more than anything else. Looking back, I believe I can more adequately answer your question from earlier. I am a man without a mother. Make of that what you will." I rose and approached the front of the cart before Dorothy could answer. "Can you take us through the gates?"

"Well…" His pause was rather concerning. Hesitation is often the prelude to no. Our ruffian here likely intended to dump us off as soon as possible and return home in hopes of securing his endless gold. "Prince Mute, won't the outskirts suffice? Forgive my craven nature, but I do not wish to linger. Your home is beautiful, my lord, but not to outsiders."

Fair enough. It really didn't matter. I would be slain immediately or not at all. The proximity of my arrival was far less important than the reaction. "Indeed. Thank you for your service. Assuming all goes to plan, I will ensure to remember…What is your name, sir?"

"Arthur, my lord." He said the words with such pride. Perhaps I underestimated the value of recognition. To be honest, it was unlikely I would remember Arthur's name over the years. But in that moment in time, I knew the man better than my own family.

"Arthur. A name I will never forget. When I return to Ganfren, I shall eagerly await my invitation to your brand-new palace."

"Um, yes, of course. Anytime."

I never expected to enjoy this man's company, or maybe—probably—I was stalling. If only horses spoke the common tongue. I would've asked them to slow down as we approached.

But perhaps they understood the sooner they arrived at the gates, the sooner I would be gone.

"This is far enough. We'll take it from here," I said, giving my escort a humble nod, then stepping off the cart. With the familiar breeze nudging through the few open spots in my mask, I was nearly relieved enough to ignore my throbbing ribs. And *oh*, how they throbbed. Whether I died immediately or gained access to a healer, either outcome would be a welcome one.

I watched Dorothy exit the cart through my peripheral vision. I could have assisted her, but chose not to. Any man who embraces sorrow can hold a grudge for a *very* long time.

"Lord Mute, I don't suppose we can skip the line?" asked Dorothy, with her arms crossed. A fair question, considering the line to enter Balewind would detain us until evening. It wasn't the amount of people—my estimate was around two hundred—but the time spent verifying each person was absurdly long. Most would be interrogated about their magic or curses to make sure no monsters like me had a chance to feel human. I suspect the guards enjoyed the authority to decide who entered and who remained in the woods. Give an insignificant man any speck of power, and watch their cruel nature grow like a weed.

"Well, I can. Not sure about you." Obviously, she couldn't see my grin. I took a few steps and waited just long enough…

"Mute!" She rushed up and grabbed my arm. "Why are you being so cross?"

The question angered me more than it should have. How could my future wife be so blind to my feelings? I was on the precipice of two fates. A loving father and king, or a noose. "The thought of not seeing my son before I die is a heavy one. There are too many moving parts, and I cannot shake the fear they are swiftly gathering around my neck. For the first time in many years, I do not yearn for the grave. Yet the moment my presence here is known, the choice will no longer be my own."

"I…My prince, before we proceed, there is something you should know about…the boy's father."

"Save it for later, Darling." Part of me knew what it was. I wager you could take a guess as well. I didn't want to ruin the lie by asking her the truth. I was content with an illusion. Fortunately, or perhaps unfortunately, denial had filled the hole in my heart left by my mother.

I ignored the line and approached the gates, also ignoring the chatter and gasps from onlookers. Some of the whispers were so loud, I could only imagine how unbearable their speaking voices would be. I wasn't sure how to make my presence known. In normal days, I could simply walk on by and receive my bows.

"A fine day for a stroll," I said to the guards. "Would you gentlemen consider parting from my path? Dorothy and I have quite the schedule ahead of us."

As much as I enjoyed silence, it didn't seem like the correct response to my question. "Mute…Lord Mute?" the lead guard said. He *very* slowly approached and said, "How can this be? The king himself proclaimed you had fallen."

"And I proclaimed it would rain today. It would seem both prophecies have failed." I considered asking if I was free to leave on my own accord, but the question wouldn't be appropriate for royalty. Inaction wasn't doing me any favors. After a pause I said, "Escort me to the king so we can share some tea. Now, if you please." Such words put the dice on their side of the gates. Any response other than "Right away, my lord" would mean betrayal. All things considered, I was oddly calm. I think, deep down, I knew I had already won.

"Forgive me, my lord, but that may not be possible."

Or not. Dorothy clutched my arm, realizing the fate I acknowledged immediately. I sighed and resisted the urge to grab my dagger. I could slay one man. Perhaps I could slay ten. I could never slay them all. Limitations to violence was always my greatest weakness.

"Oh? What a pity. I suppose I did all this work and secured tradelines for no reason. Would you prefer to rush me at once or is it easier to wait for an army?"

"What? My lord…Ah, of course, you wouldn't know. King Merrick Elmere is ill. Deathly ill, I'm afraid. Forgive me for being crass but, to be quite honest, your presence here is a miracle. Come! I will escort you to the castle immediately. And who is this?"

I was too flustered to tell this nameless soldier he was addressing my queen. The king…Brother Dearest…ill? Deathly ill? My first thought was perhaps this man was uneducated, but the uneducated ones were never designated to the gates. No one says "deathly ill" by mistake. Right?

So I followed. What else could I do? It was the sort of pitfall where any questions would only lead to more questions. I barely noticed Dorothy take my arm. She whispered, "My condolences, Lord Mute."

"Hold your tongue." Rude? Yes, but I didn't know how to feel or how to react. This was good. This was good…right? Brother could die without me ever dirtying my blade. Lector would be all the happier. In fact, he would probably believe I was a genius for slaying Merrick without raising a finger. But it was wrong! Oh, so wrong. What a cruel joke after years of wishing ill upon the man. For some of us, the worst fate imaginable is to have our prayers answered.

"My lord," the guard said, as we walked through the city streets. "Forgive me for asking above my station, but are the rumors true? We heard foreigners murdered the duke, then you were captured defending him."

"Pardon?" In hindsight, I shouldn't have spoken at all. Still, the tale had caught me off guard. To arm myself with a lie only to face an unexpected one changed the course of everything. "Who told you this?"

"It's the official story from King Merrick himself. Did I…leave out any important details?"

My long pause may have tipped him off. If it did, he was smart enough not to push the issue farther. "None. I'm just surprised to hear an accurate account of the evening. My uncle, the lord duke, he died a brave man. May his name live forever in our hearts." There was a joy to lying. A strange, intimate secret between me and my scoundrel uncle, who was most likely rotting in hell.

"Well said, my lord."

It must have been, for it was the last thing any of us said until we reached the castle.

CHAPTER II

A Man With Nothing To Hide

 had always feared my brother, and never understood why. Even as a child, I was taller, better-read, had better knowledge of exotic wines, a bigger chest, bigger arms. You get the idea. Still, to the realm, Merrick was immaculate. God-like. An enchanter of crowds, a dazzler of women. Everything I was supposed to be and more.

Or at least, he had been.

Who was this man lying in bed within his chambers, surrounded by scented candles? His hair was still long and blonde, but it was thin. His face was thin. His eyes were thin. I imagined his very soul was thin, if he still had one.

"Do you require a moment alone?" asked Dorothy.

I had nearly forgotten she was there. I squeezed her hand—far too hard in hindsight—and said, "No. Please, no. Not now." I was too weak to face Merrick alone. In reality, I had been too weak to face most of the problems of my life alone, but no one had bothered to stay by my side after Mother's departure.

Brother Dearest gave a slight cough, which quickly became a hack. "Mute…It's you. It's really you, isn't it? And look! You brought your whore. The one…who ruined everything."

I took a deep breath to compose myself, impressed at

Dorothy's lack of reaction. Though I was rather sad that she was used to hearing such insults. "Her name is Dorothy, Your *Royal Highness.*"

"I know her fucking name." To my dismay, he forced himself out of bed. Without the illusion of covers, I saw everything above the waist. Every bone, every sore. A corpse that shivered and clutched his robes. "Was it worth it, Brother? That's all I wish to know."

"Yes," I said immediately, to my own surprise. While lies take time to conjure, the truth is always there, stewing in our hearts, waiting to be unleashed.

"The greatest liars are the ones that fool themselves. Come forth. Allow me to look at her. Let me see the harlot that shattered a kingdom."

I kept my head down and froze. There would always be something about my brother's commands that sent ice down my spine. There had been a time—not a long one—where I eagerly answered his beck and call. Sadly enough, those had been the best days of my life.

Dorothy was well-trained enough not to react as he touched her face. It resembled nothing of an intimate gesture, more like an architect studying a stone. "So plain. So common. So utterly forgettable. I'll never understand what he sees in you. I suppose, in a way, it is what separates us."

"I can name at least one more thing," I said, tapping the edge of my mask. "Brother, I did not come here to stir trouble. I had no idea about…this. Any of this."

Brother coughed again, away from the direction of Dorothy. "Funny you should say that. I have been trying to fill in the missing piece of the puzzle. I figured those heathens in Ganfren would make you their carnival freak or some abhorrent fate. Why are you here? Why are you *alive?*"

So many lies rushed up at once. I pushed them all aside and

remembered the one that had gotten me this far. "I was tortured thoroughly the first few days. Or at least, I believe it was days. Always difficult to tell when the sun and moon converge into layers of darkness. Several blades later, they realized a man with no knowledge is a man with nothing to hide. Then, Brother Dearest, after some time to break bread, they offered me this."

I dumped my pack onto the ground and picked up the paper nearest to the top. "Tradelines. The Dilfoy connection. I did it, Brother. I didn't even realize I was on a mission, but as always, I served the crown with pride." My eyes filled with tears, both out of shame and relief. My mask usually didn't work on Merrick. He saw everything.

Brother appeared dumbfounded as he gazed upon the treaty. If I had known any better, I would have assumed the man was in a state of unparalleled terror. After an uncomfortable pause, he said, "Oh, Mute. It fills my heart with joy to know you're alive."

Was that an apology? Or merely a declaration? He obviously knew that I knew he was lying. But did he know I was lying? I would test the waters. "Indeed. How I wish Uncle was here to revel in our victory together."

"Don't overplay your hand. There is only one card above the king, and I assure you, it doesn't wear a mask."

"Then I lay my cards upon the table. Why did you do it? I gave you my heart, Brother. Even after you and Father took everything from me. I still gave you whatever was left, even if it was only a variation of nothing."

Instead of an answer, Brother grabbed a decanter of wine from his dresser and chugged the entire thing. He then opened one of the drawers and took out a tiny bag of white powder. I refuse to describe the awful sound his nose made as he sniffed it all up. I was no healing mage, but these actions seemed rather unwise for a man nearing his own end. Or maybe that was the point. If death was inevitable, it may as well come while he felt nothing.

"Duke Gunther made a play to become king," Dorothy said. "He couldn't stop bragging about it that night…"

"Silence, whore!" Brother yelled, causing me to flinch. Uncle had been the betrayer? Why? There was too much to take in at once. I considered using the Gift of Silence, if only to give myself a moment with my thoughts.

If the words had any effect on Dorothy, nothing could be seen on her face. "You sent Mute to Eleanor's to slay Archibald, then you sent me to the duke for…entertainment, knowing our paths would cross. Was that the plan? To kill them both in one evening?"

"I nearly did," Brother said with a chuckle. "And I don't even care that I failed. Fuck Uncle Gunther. Fuck him to the very depths of hell." Brother cleared his nose, which was one of the most unpleasant sounds I ever heard. "My…let's be diplomatic and call it a problem…was becoming impossible to hide. Uncle said if I conspired with Ganfren to eliminate Mute, he would wait until my natural end before usurping the throne. A clean succession, he called it. Why wouldn't I agree? Tomorrow is ages away for an addict. Everything—past, present, future—it all converges on the now."

Even with my mask I felt naked. "How was I a threat? I don't even want the throne." But I did, and perhaps I always did. Maybe everyone saw it but me. I changed the subject to avoid either of them calling out my lie. "Brother…what happened to you? What would Mother say if she saw you now?"

Brother slowly approached. He placed a hand on my mask and stared straight into my eyes. "Forgive me, Orion, my sweet older brother. For years I battled my demons. I did not win."

I was too stunned to react. Too stunned to prevent him from walking out of his chambers. Dorothy and I stood there alone, in complete silence, our minds desperately trying to piece together theories on what to do next. It didn't take long for me to choose. "Take our son and flee Balewind. Before you ask where, I don't know. Not here. Anywhere is safer than here."

Dorothy sighed. "My son has resided in Balewind Castle for years in the lower chambers with the serving staff. King Merrick never made any outright threats, but it was obviously implied. As far as I am concerned, *here* is the only place for me. Lord Mute, do you plan to stay in the castle?"

"I have nowhere else to go." And it was true. Even if this castle was meant to be my grave, at least I would die at home.

"Then we share the same fate. I do not believe your brother is bold enough to attack you in the open. Tensions are high enough with your unexpected return."

Underestimating the boldness of a man snorting powder on his deathbed didn't seem like a rational course of action. Was it odd I didn't want Dorothy by my side? To be painfully honest, I was tired of the people I loved treating me like a tool. "Come," I said, because I didn't know what else to do. Not even I could leave her there alone. If I must be a tool, I could at least choose to be a shield.

I nodded to the door and left. She followed of course, having enough courtesy not to take my arm. Home was familiar, but it was still a dreamy haze. It felt like I was walking through a memory that wasn't my own, a faded echo of better days, a remnant of a time long lost. Fortunately, my room was only a few steps down the hallway. I pushed open the doors, half expecting an assassin to pop out and stab me through the neck.

But nothing happened. I glanced around and it was just how I remembered it. Even the glass of water on my dresser was still half-empty. "Rest," I said, nodding to the other side of my bed. Hopefully, she would take it as a command and not a suggestion. I was too tired to argue.

"What about you? We should take turns keeping lookout."

"Rest, Darling. If there are any dangers, I shall protect you from them." She could probably tell I was lying, though I didn't care.

"Lord Mute, while I admire your honor and tenacity, I cannot help but wonder if our best course of action would be to—"

"I know the boy isn't mine. But it gave me something to live for. Something…a reason to keep going. I worship lies the way my brother worships his powder." A long pause followed. Perhaps Dorothy was debating whether to continue lying, but silence made the decision for her.

"I'm sorry."

"Not nearly as much as I am. Now rest. I will hear no more of this. Perhaps I will hear no more of anything."

Another pause. It's a marvel how long silence can stretch time. "I was going to tell you eventually. You must understand, I feared for my life. I didn't know you as I do now. You fall…somewhere between a good man and a decent one. Not a monster."

I wished she would stop speaking or, at the very least, stop lying. It was insufferable. Part of me considered using the Gift of Silence. It would've brought an end to the lies, and probably my own life, soon after. "Oh, Darling, I could never harm you. Not even now."

"Lord Mute, does that mean…are we on good terms?"

No. We weren't. I took a deep breath as my hands went to the latch on the back of my mask. With a click, it came off, then I turned and faced her. "You are the only woman I ever loved. And I can never forgive you for that."

I lay down and put my mask on the side of the bed. Really, I'm not sure what I expected after those words. I knew Dorothy hadn't wronged me. We don't choose who we love. We don't choose what we favor. If we did, the world would be all the more simple, and all the less beautiful. It's all some strange amalgamation of chaos and nature.

Dorothy never answered. She drifted off to sleep on her side of the bed, breathing in and out quietly. For many, many, years, I had dreamed of this moment. Dorothy here, in my bed, sleeping next to me with no mask between us. My prayers were answered, and I had never been less happy.

Perhaps it was a sign to stop praying for things.

CHAPTER 12

KING-IN-STANDING

s it still a lie when you attempt to fulfill a promise but ultimately fail? I could only wonder as I woke in my bed, alone. I had sworn to Dorothy I would stay awake and protect her, but my body and fatigue had colluded against me. Sunlight crept through the window. Apparently, I had slept for a while. Much longer than anticipated—but not forever, which was a tiny victory.

I rose and put my mask back on, deciding no one would ever see my face again. Like most of my proclamations, it was done in silence. I wasn't exactly sure what to do next. Forgive me for being blunt, but I had hoped one of my brother's assassins would make the decision for me. After a pause, I nudged open my chamber doors and stepped outside, half expecting an ensemble of guards to finish the job.

"A fine morning, my lord," a random guard said.

"Salutations, Lord Mute," a cleaning lady said.

I was more confused than disappointed. Was the plan to ignore reality and carry on as if nothing had happened? Fine. I could play that game. I had dabbled in denial long before these folk. My newfound determination faded as I passed Brother's chambers. I did not know if he was in there. To be honest, I wasn't even sure he was still alive—

I lost my breath as a hand grabbed my shoulder. This was it. I was going to die. In that moment, I'm not too proud to admit pain was what I feared most of all. It's easy to speak a tough game when it comes to murder. Let me tell you: death is often painful. Despite the silence, I could always see it in their eyes. See it in the way their throat strained in horror. Attempting to describe a scream with your eyes is not a pleasant task.

"Oh, you're tense. Relax, Brother. Or should I say, Your Majesty?"

Lost for words, I turned around and faced Merrick. His smile was filled with daggers, though, fortunately, his hands were not. "Perhaps I need a cup of morning tea, for I certainly misheard you."

"Not this time. Father always taught me never to waste bad luck. For the rest of the week, I have informed the royal council you will be their king-in-standing. Don't worry, I'm sure you'll do just a *fine* job. Even you can't be worse than Aunty. A woman on the throne. Of all the indecencies…"

He walked away before I could respond. Apparently, Brother had gotten quite good at that. Was he mad? Well, maybe. He certainly was not in peak mental condition, though I dare not guess where the line between madness and fatigue lies. Even if it was only for a second, I wished I could have believed his intentions were good. To mock your sibling loses dignity after a certain age.

So, I entered the throne room. Really, where else could I go? Silence followed my arrival as the doors opened. Everyone immediately stared in my direction. Who was that on the throne? I squinted to get a better look…Oh. Aunty Alexandra. Gunther's wife. That could be problematic. I had made her a widow and, apparently, a temporary queen.

If there was any venom in her heart, none appeared on her

face. She smiled at me and said, "Ah, Your Majesty. Such timing is fortuitous. General Weston and I were just discussing the encampment of Southern thieves down by the lake. There are two strategies on the table. Perhaps you could offer some fresh perspective? Gods know I tire of the role."

Adrenaline coursed through my blood from hearing the words "Your Majesty." Such a title could never be spoken in error. To be king was to hold unlimited power, and I wanted that power. I *needed* that power. If I couldn't hold the people's love, their obedience would have to suffice. The duchess moved out of my way as I sat on the throne. It was far from comfortable, but I would find relief in time. I imagined it was like getting used to wearing a mask.

I leaned back and said, "Thieves, you say? I fail to see the impasse. Remind me, how do we deal with thieves, General?"

His eyes grew bright, clearly appreciating the fact he had an ally in the crown. "In all my years, I have only known one way, Your Majesty."

"Then do it, and leave their corpses as tribute for Lepock. The Silent God despises thieves."

"*My lord!*" the general—and pretty much everyone else— yelled in unison. I had committed blasphemy, a mortal sin, a crime Father had hung entire families for. And I didn't care in the slightest. Once you call someone "Your Majesty," you ascend them to a level which should not exist. Such ascension is irreversible, minus a blade or a poison.

"Henceforth, to speak the Silent God's name is no longer a crime. In fact, I encourage it. All of my life, I was told I had a curse. Some…aberration that prevented me from becoming king. Yet here I am, sitting on the throne of my forefathers. The future may not be loud but, I assure you, it will be bright."

No one cheered. Perhaps I had overplayed my hand and moved too quickly, especially with Merrick still alive. Could they see the sweat pouring behind my mask? Authority is an illusion when there is no way to enforce it.

My general eventually broke the silence. He bowed and said, "Very well, Your Majesty. Consider it done."

And that was it. I had declared a law, and in doing so, I had made my supremacy known for all who would listen. A tad ironic, considering I planned to be the silent king.

I won't bore you with the rest. The room filled, and all sorts of people took the opportunity to address their king-in-standing and harass me with various problems. I denied most of them. Not out of spite, but because I hadn't the slightest clue on how much gold my kingdom wielded. I hadn't the slightest clue about our military structure. I hadn't the slightest clue about the slightest clue.

Hours later, my lower half was sore as I rose from the throne. While most of the room had cleared out, Duchess Alexandra remained. She glared at me. The way her smile regressed into a scowl was a magic that put my silence to shame. "I only have one question, Orion. What were his dying words?"

The question caught me off guard to say the least. I scanned both her hands for blades and found nothing. "Who?"

She scoffed. "Don't play coy. Who do you think? My husband. Your *uncle*."

It was incredibly rude for me to chuckle. It wasn't intentional, of course, but the question was hilarious in a strange way. "Sorry, Love. Couldn't hear a thing." Was it worth telling Aunty how her husband had fondled Dorothy? I opted not to. I thoroughly believe every woman possesses a power that informs them when their lover betrays them.

"How unfortunate. I hope he screamed."

"Well, he certainly tried to."

The duchess sighed, but I caught hints of a smile. Believe me, I always check. "May Lepock take him, Your Majesty."

CHAPTER 13

HEAVEN

h, what a lovely day. I casually strolled throughout the castle, making my way towards Brother's chambers. Was it to gloat? Yes, of course it was. I didn't bother to knock, instead, flinging the doors open with a wide grin.

My grin vanished when I saw him lying there, surrounded by servants. "Miserable whore!" he yelled, flinging a chalice that barely missed a young girl's skull. "I said I was hot! Does hot require more blankets? What brothel did you crawl out from? Get out of my sight!" Tears fell from the girl's eyes as she ran out the door. She forgot to bow in my presence, but I wouldn't hold it against her. This time, at least.

Brother stopped yelling, seemingly content to devour his bread. Can you love a person and still wish them harm? For whatever reason, the sight of Merrick chomping down food with his mouth wide open begged the question. "Leave us," he managed between bites, waving the other two girls away. He glanced at the window and said, "About time you slithered in here. I half expected you to run after your whore."

I shrugged, resisting the urge to smile. Even with my mask, I knew he would see it. "Well, Brother Dearest, someone has to play king."

"What?" At least that caught his attention. He threw the remaining bread on the floor and coughed. "You were bold enough to face Aunty? Perhaps I was mistaken. That Dorothy girl is good for your nerves. Where did she run off to? Whatever you may believe, I was never going to harm her. Unlike someone in this room, I cannot fathom what it's like to hurt family."

"For the first time in my life, I can honestly say I don't care. Oh, forgot to mention, I legalized speaking the Silent God's name out loud. *Lepock.* Has a ring to it, wouldn't you agree? Lepock. Lepock, Lepock."

"Stop! You fool! What madness has befallen you? Speak that name in my presence again and I swear—brother or not—I shall bury you in a silent grave."

"You tried that already. Whether skill or good fortune, I still remain. Times are changing, Brother Dearest. Now that I had a taste, I desire what has always been mine by birthright. I offer you the same deal Uncle did. I will bide my time in the shadows while you sniff and drink your way to oblivion. But when the time is right, Balewind will fall under the authority of the silent king."

"Balewind will indeed fall." After an award pause, Brother laughed, which was about the last thing I expected. "You speak a fair game for a silent man. You can't kill me, can you? Believe me, the weakness lingers in my own blood as well. I blame Mother. She always…the way she spoke about you. It made me…Why are you here, Mute? Why are you alive?" He rose from the bed and slowly approached.

"I don't know. I haven't known for a long time." There was no point in lying anymore. You can't bluff when your opponent sees your hand. "Lector Shaw sent me here to kill you, but I apparently share your weakness in that regard."

"And why is that? Honor? Brotherly love? Spare me such nonsense. If Father had just drowned you in the lake, none of this would have happened. I spit on his weakness."

"Mother…"

"Ah, yes. Mother. It always comes back to Mother. That's about the time you cracked, wasn't it? A pity Father didn't bed someone more worthy. True, it would probably mean I never entered the realm, but I still believe it would be worth it just to never see that fucking mask again."

Why was he speaking this way? We had been there together at her funeral. We had both cried to the point of wailing. Me, holding my little brother, and him, clutching my waist with all his tiny strength. Unable to figure it out, I did something bold. Something foolish.

I embraced my brother, cleared my mind, and closed my eyes. "*Hush*," I whispered, then the castle went deaf.

With all his muscles gone, we hugged like we were children again. I cannot say how much time passed, but each fading second may as well have been forever. The moment would have been more intimate if Brother hadn't grabbed the dagger out of my sheath and pressed it against my neck. The shock caught me off guard, sending me to the ground. He was barely a pack of bones, but he used his weight efficiently, crushing my shoulder and keeping the blade in position. With the way his hands shook, I did not expect to remain in this realm very long. And that would be okay.

"I don't remember her face," he said, clearly enough for me to read his lips. "Why can't I remember her face? You were always her favorite, Orion. In killing you, she will reveal herself to me. I will join you in heaven soon enough. And when I do, I'll describe her to you. Every detail, every hair on her head."

Heaven. That word would always wound my heart. I already knew I would never enter heaven. Even if one ignored all of my murders, I had entered Eleanor's brothel, and such a toll must always be paid.

I grabbed Brother's hands after a small laceration opened on my neck. With his tiny frame, I easily pushed him back and mounted him, knocking the dagger several feet away. I wish I hadn't done that. Daggers are good for a quick, clean death. Hands, however, not so much.

I grabbed his neck. It was thin enough to get my hands all the way around. I clenched as hard as I could, begging the Gift of Silence to spare me his cries. If his legs were flailing, I could not hear them bang upon the ground. If my hands crushed his neck, not a crack was made. If I cried, not a whimper was heard.

I swear, before his end, he managed to mouth, "Brother, what happened to us? We were supposed to live forever…"

But he didn't live forever. He was dead. He was dead and, yet, I kept squeezing. To this day, I don't know why. The only reason I eventually stopped was because a guard grabbed me and threw me to the side. And the side was where I remained. Obviously, I couldn't hear a thing, but it didn't take sound to watch the guard feel for a pulse and find nothing. He shrugged to Aunty, who turned to me and smiled.

"Well done, my king."

CHAPTER 14

THE WHISPER THAT REPLACED GOD

he plan had been to lay in bed and never sleep again. That plan had failed. Unlike most of my dreams, I was already sitting on the throne with a glowing dagger. Odd as it was, the fact my mask reflected in the steel instead of my actual face was more so. I flinched as hands grabbed my shoulder. It wasn't the shock or the power, but merely the fact they were so cold.

I never understood dreams. Perhaps because gods never sleep. Gods never slumber. You did well to invoke my name, my silent little prince. There will come a time when the last mortal voice speaks their final word. Not in your lifetime, of course. Not in your children's lifetime. But it will come. When it does, I will finally know silence. It will be an indescribable euphoria. Thank you, Orion. Anytime you struggle to find meaning, remember that all of this is because of you.

All of this is because of you.

I was no longer sure if it was a dream. The Silent God's voice pressed against my skull, filling me with a physical pain that normally never occurred in these visions. I tried to wake. You know the motions: blinking, slapping, sudden movements. I'm not ashamed to say it was terrifying. Perhaps I had died and hadn't realized it. That would be a fitting end after what I had done to Brother—

She was coming. Mother was coming. She walked down the aisle towards my throne. I doubled my efforts to wake. I even pressed my nails deep into my wrist. It didn't work. Nothing worked.

Up close, I saw everything. And more importantly, I *remembered* everything. I refuse to describe it. Say what you will, but some memories are too intimate to share with strangers. Mother was terrible. Mother was beautiful. Mother was everything. "It's you," I said with a smile. A true smile, the sort that came in those few moments when life was grand. "Mother, I remember everything."

"Good. Take a gander, my son. You will never see me again."

I nearly collapsed but I gripped my armrest. "No! You can't leave me. Not now. Not after everything."

"In taking your brother's life, you have pushed me away forever. I never wished for this, but the river of life flows as it will. There is only so much we can do to our loved ones before they wither away into dust."

"*No!*" I rose from my throne and looked down. This wasn't real. None of it was real. Dreams could never harm me. "I will hear no more of this. Not even from you. Say goodbye if you must, but don't torment me. Please don't torment me." I didn't want to hear goodbye, but the thought of never hearing her voice again was nearly as terrible. Enough. I was better than this. If silence was my fate, it would come on my own terms.

I closed my eyes, cleared my mind, and focused on nothing. "*Hush*," I whispered, then …

Something was wrong. The comfort of silence was nowhere to be found. I didn't dare speak out loud. Did the spell fail? Impossible. Mother slowly ascended the stairs towards my throne. Despite my gift, I heard every frantic breath come and go from my body.

Mother smiled as she grabbed my shoulders and gently pulled me in. "This is a nightmare, Deary. Your magic doesn't work here."

"Don't leave me," I whispered, holding back tears. "Or better yet, take me with you. Take me with you, Mother. I don't wish to be here anymore."

"I don't know what to say. You're too old to rely on a mother's lies. What did Dorothy tell you? Somewhere between a decent man and a good one? There are worse fates, my son. You will persevere. It will be difficult. It will be painful, but you will persevere."

"Why am I the only one left?"

Mother shook her head. "You had a brother, in case you forgot. He was not wise; he was not compassionate, but he was…well, he was my boy. In a better realm, Merrick would've been the perfect king."

"There was a time where I saw him as God."

"Such a time has come to an end. For better or for worse, that role is yours now. You are the whisper that replaced God."

"Oh, Mother. What happened to me? I woke up one day and life had passed me by. I wish…I could go back. Fix all of it. Fix any of it, really. Or maybe just…forget a day or two."

"I'm afraid nothing strengthens memories more than sorrow and regret. Now give me a kiss. The world is going to be a difficult place when you wake, but never forget how much I love you. If it's any consolation, I killed your father. You are not alone in your shame. We are lost, Orion. We are all so very lost."

I felt her fade from my grasp. To my shock, I did not weep. Actually, I didn't do anything. I went numb. Both in the physical sense…and the other senses I don't feel like describing.

Waking from that dream was the sort of pain we only wish on our worst enemies.

CHAPTER 15

MELANCHOLY

 elancholy is a fascinating word. Ask any ten people for a definition, and I wager ten entirely unique descriptions of despair will follow. My opinion? Melancholy is the window to the soul: that tiny spot between depression and normality where most of us linger. One man's low is another man's high. I have seen people driven to madness by the slightest of troubles, while mothers bury their children with no more than a single tear. In a way, I envy them both.

Sorry, I should mention that quite some time had passed. Not sure how much, really. Less than decades, more than years, but it may as well have been eons upon eons. It all blends together after a while. Life as king had been more lonely than one would imagine. Being surrounded by people doesn't seem to matter when none of them see you as a fellow human. An ironic fate. I had dared to become God, then wept as heaven became a prison of my own construct.

Every morning, every night, I had waited for an assassination. For some hero to slay me in the name of honor and justice. Perhaps yearned would be the better word. When Aunty had died, I was disappointed. She had seen who or what I was—and she accepted me! The man behind the mask. The so-called monster. When

King Lector Shaw had died, I realized my disappointment would be permanent. Oh, the dread of knowing nothing was coming. While it's only natural to fear change, there is nothing worse than permanent stagnation.

And permanent stagnation it was. I stood upon the balcony. It was rather awkward to take my brother's chambers after sending him to the grave, but I spent most nights in that dreary place. There, the wind was but a melancholy whisper. An invisible hand, nudging me through the echoes of life, straight into that time where it was too cold to be spring, but memories of winter had long melted between my fingers.

I never dreamed of Mother again, despite how much I yearned to. It would seem trying to force people into dreams is the quickest way to ensure they never come. Still, I never forgot her face. For all the prices I had paid on my journey to the throne, that one at least offered solace. I never saw Dorothy again either. That one hurt more than I'm willing to express with words. All I can hope for is that she eventually found happiness by escaping me. There are few things worse than knowing someone you love is better off without you.

As always, after a time, I left the balcony and entered the throne room. It was strange to sit upon my throne while the darkness of midnight crept through the windows. The sight of it used to scare me. I had believed an empty throne room meant a dying kingdom, or something of the sort. The only thing dead now was my outlook for tomorrow. For all my troubles, for all my woes, very little inspired fear anymore. No, it's not that I grew brave, but the disease of apathy had spread from my heart to my soul. I was poisoned. Oh, so very poisoned.

Am I rambling? Sorry, I may be rambling. It's awkward to end my adventure this way. Normally, the hero would slay a dragon, a monster, or some deranged god wearing a sun mask. But most stories that never get told involve someone battling the demons created within their own heart. If my family was any indication, the hero tends to lose those battles in a slow, agonizing defeat.

I had myself, my thoughts and…more time than I could possibly imagine. Heed my words: even an inquisitor would blush at the idea of too much time. Was Dorothy out there, thinking of me? Waiting for me? No, probably not. I doubt anyone did. All I had now were my thoughts.

And to be alone with my thoughts was just another form of being alone.

THANK YOU FOR READING!

If you happened to enjoy this novella, feel free to pick up my epic fantasy trilogy: The Legacy of Boulom, featuring Platinum Tinted Darkness, Tears of the Maelstrom, and Age of Arrogance.

Willow Wraith Press is a collective of nerds who write the types of books we want to read. If you have enjoyed this book, please check out the other Willow Wraiths.

Dewey Conway & Bill Adams:

The Tenacious Tale of Tanna the Tendersword

Bill Adams:

The Godsblood Tragedy

Andrew D. Meredith:

Deathless Beast
Bone Shroud
Gloves of Eons

Thrice
Four Scored

Quaint Creatures: Magical & Mundane

Michael Roberti:

The Traitors We Are
A Grave for Us All
The Revenge of Thousands

Timothy Wolff:

Platinum Tinted Darkness
Tears of the Maelstrom
Age of Arrogance

The Whisper that Replaced God

MEET THE AUTHOR

Timothy Wolff lives in Long Island, New York, and holds a master's degree in economics and a career in finance. Such a life has taught him the price of everything but the value of nothing. He enjoys pizza bagels, scotch, karaoke, oxford commas, and spending the day with family and friends. The obvious culmination of the past thirty-six years was to write a 400+ page fantasy novel where a drunk teams up with a swordsman, two mages, and lizard-people to oppose god. Why do we write these in the third person?

Strength without honor—is chaos!

He can be reached at:

@TimWolffAuthor on Twitter, X, or whatever the hell the site is called by the time this book is published.

Timwolffauthor on Instagram/Threads

timwolffauthor@gmail.com

THANKS, ACKNOWLEDGEMENTS, ETC.

Yeah this book is a weird one. The idea for Mute and the first chapter came to me in the shower. I figured it could be an interesting trilogy. Then I thought maybe an interesting standalone novel. Settled on novella. It's possible one day I will revisit this world, though I will say, being in Mute's head is a strange place.

As always, first thanks go to my immediate family of Joan, Larry, and Danny, who have always been super supportive despite not being fans of the fantasy genre. After two years, I'm proud to announce my brother has finished Chapter 1 of *Platinum Tinted Darkness*. I usually don't thank my extended family in fear of missing someone, but I do want to extend a special thanks to my cousin, Kelsey.

Special thanks to my two beta readers: Amber Lilyquist and J. Flowers-Olnowich. I really can't exaggerate how important it is to have good beta readers who won't hesitate to be like "hey, I like it, but this part literally makes no sense." And of course my editor, Jon Oliver who has fixed the horrors of my comma and semicolon usage for four books now, and overall is an awesome dude.

Anyone who follows my work probably knows all my covers are done by Alejandro Colucci. Aside from being one of the nicest people I've ever worked with, his ability to turn my unhinged descriptions into something amazing is a skill I will forever envy.

The indie fantasy community has been amazing. I always found "no one writes alone" to be a cliché, but I now swear by it. Writing can be brutal at times. Sometimes the words don't come.

Sometimes the words come and they are very bad. The community is a blessing, and I am forever grateful for all the people I met in the past two years. Forgive me skipping names, but I don't want to miss anyone. I think you know who you are.